Looking for Juliette

A Richard Jackson Book

INVESTIGATORS OF THE UNKNOWN
BOOK TWO

Looking
for
Juliette

Janet Taylor Lisle

Orchard Books • New York

Orchard Books
95 Madison Avenue, New York, NY 10016

Manufactured in the United States of America
Book design by Mina Greenstein
The text of this book is set in 12 point New Aster.
1   3   5   7   9   10   8   6   4   2

Library of Congress Cataloging-in-Publication Data
Lisle, Janet Taylor.
   Looking for Juliette / Janet Taylor Lisle.
   p.   cm. — (Investigators of the unknown ; bk. 2)
   "A Richard Jackson book"—T.p. verso.
   Summary: When Angela moves away for a year,
   her best friends Poco and Georgina and a
   mysterious classmate are convinced that the
   elderly Miss Bone, caretaker of Angela's
   house, is responsible for the
   inexplicable disappearance of her cat.
ISBN 0-531-06870-6.   ISBN 0-531-08720-4 (lib. bdg.)
   [1. Supernatural—Fiction.   2. Cats—Fiction.
   3. Old age—Fiction.   4. Friendship—Fiction.]
   I. Title.   II. Series: Lisle, Janet Taylor.
   Investigators of the unknown ; bk. 2.
            PZ7.L6912Lo   1994
            [Fic]—dc20   94-6922

Looking for Juliette

One

GEORGINA RUSK and Poco Lambert were shocked when their friend Angela Harrall told them the news. She had only just found out herself, from her mother at breakfast that very Saturday morning.

"You're moving!" Georgina screeched. They were all up in her room, sitting on the bed. "But Angela, how can you? What will you do without us!"

"I suppose I'll think of something," Angela replied with a little sniff. "I won't just dry up and blow away, if that's what you mean."

"That *is* what I mean!" Georgina couldn't help

saying. "We are the three best friends in the entire universe!"

It was true. All that fall they had been cosmic friends. They had spent afternoons doing their homework at one another's houses and Friday nights going to the movies. They had played slapjack in Poco's kitchen and practiced calligraphy in Angela's with her father's special pen.

They had pooled their money to buy a bottle of rather expensive blue nail polish and painted their fingernails and toes. Afterward, since he seemed to be looking on so eagerly from his cage, Poco had painted Edward's whiskers. He was Georgina's hamster.

"Edward has always secretly wished for blue whiskers," Poco explained. "You know, like Bluebeard the Pirate? Bluebeard is his hero. He told me."

"Bluebeard the Pirate! Edward?" cried Georgina, who did not believe in pets having conversations with people. She frowned at Poco. "Why is it that this hamster only speaks to *you*? When there are so many other persons around he could speak to? Including *me*, his owner?"

"I'm sorry, George, but I have no control over these things," Poco had replied in an insulted voice. "I'll mention it to Edward the next time we talk."

Cosmic as they were, the friends did not always get along. They were separate people with separate views of the world, so what could one expect? About the main things, though, they tended to agree, and that fall, more than anything else, they had agreed on the existence of magic.

Magic. The word made their eyes darken and grow watchful. This was not the toy store variety sold in boxes. Real magic appeared where it was least expected, they knew, and then evaporated like mist before the hand could grasp it. It hid out in the ordinary and often managed to explain itself in ways that sounded completely reasonable. To catch magic at work, you had to be patient. You had to keep a sharp eye and a trusting mind. Only then would clues begin to show up—a puff of gold dust, strange lights in the hall—evidence that other powers, somewhere, were alive. Angela's gold dust letters had revealed many things. The friends had been on the verge of discovering more when . . .

"Angela Harrall, I order you to stay!" Georgina yelled, stamping her foot so hard that Edward was rattled awake in his cage. He poked his blue whiskers out the front of his little house and stared at them with worried black eyes.

Poco said nothing. She dropped down on Georgina's bed and curled into a ball, like one of those furry caterpillars found along the roadside at that time of the year.

"Poco! For goodness' sake. Get up and do something!" Georgina cried. "Angela is going to South America."

"To Mexico," Angela said, looking a bit shaken herself. "My father needs to be near his business there. My brother, Martin, is going, too. We'll be back in a year."

"A year!" Georgina clenched her fists. "What about your mother?"

"Oh, she's decided to move to California for a while. She's thinking of going to law school."

Everyone knew that Angela's parents didn't live together anymore, though they weren't yet actually divorced.

"My mom will come and visit us a lot, and we'll fly up and visit her," Angela went on bravely. "It won't be so bad. I'll go to a school where I'll learn to speak Spanish."

This was too much for Georgina. With a wild

leap, she hurled herself onto the bed beside Poco. "Spanish!" she shrieked. "But what about us?"

Poco had begun to uncurl by this time. She sat up and turned to Angela with a serious expression on her face.

"What is going to happen to Juliette?" she asked. Juliette, the Harrall family's big Siamese cat, was a special friend of hers.

"I don't know." Angela shrugged. "We haven't talked about it."

"She won't like Mexico," Poco said. "Too hot. And the mice have tropical diseases."

"Maybe she should stay here, then."

"I think she should." Poco raised her tiny eyebrows. "If she would like a place to stay, my house is available."

"I'll ask my mother," Angela answered. "It sounds like a good idea."

"No, it doesn't," screamed Georgina, who was not one to make changes without a great deal of fuss. "It sounds like the worst idea I've ever heard. Juliette will run away! Also, who will take care of your house? And you can't just drop out of school. The teachers will be furious after all the time they've already wasted on you."

Angela, who had been gazing fondly at Georgina during most of this tirade, narrowed her eyes when it came to the part about the teachers. A dark red flush appeared on her cheeks.

"Please don't worry, George," she replied through thin lips. "Everything will be taken care of. Miss Bone is going to look after our house."

"Miss Bone! Who is she? We've never even met her, have we?"

"She will be there whether you've met her or not," Angela said. "And I will be in Mexico, so that's the end of that!"

○

IMPOSSIBLE as it seemed, Angela and her family were gone less than a month later. Their clothes were packed, their suitcases were shipped off, and a black limousine came and rushed them away to the airport.

After a brief flurry of gardeners and cleaning people, the Harrall residence was deserted. The big house was closed up. Curtains were drawn. Lights burned in odd places, even during the day. Poco and Georgina couldn't help going by on their walks home from school.

As the days passed, a queer emptiness took hold of the yard. The trees looked barer, the bushes more forlorn. Even the little creatures that come and go so busily around a normal, lived-in house seemed, one by one, to disappear.

There were no squirrels in the trees, Poco noticed after the second week. Few birds came to roost on the house's broad roof. The mouse-sized moles that had tunneled so relentlessly into the front lawn and driven poor Mrs. Harrall to distraction went away. A family of rabbits nesting in one of the side hedges moved out.

The reasonable explanation for these disappearances was certainly that winter had come. It was November. Most birds had flown south. Many animals were digging down into the earth or building homes in more protected places. Poco knew this, and yet . . .

"No dogs walk through the yard anymore," she pointed out to Georgina one day. "The fat groundhog is gone from under the apple tree. I have the strangest feeling that Angela's house is being avoided."

"I've noticed that somebody is living in the apartment over the garage," Georgina replied.

"There are lights on up there every night, and a car is parked outside one of the doors sometimes."

"It's Miss Bone." Poco frowned. "She's living there while she looks after the house. My mother said she used to be a teacher at the high school. Now she's too old and does housesitting jobs."

"Miss Bone," Georgina mused. "That's a strange name."

"Sort of horrible when you think of it," Poco agreed.

The most important animal missing from the Harrall house and garden was, of course, Juliette. There was nothing odd about this, however. The big Siamese was staying with Poco while the Harralls were away, an arrangement that seemed to make everyone happy.

Angela had an excuse to call up from Mexico, so the friends, who were not great letter writers, could stay in touch. Meanwhile, Poco had a sleeping companion at last. Every night Juliette curled up on the foot of her bed, just as she had used to snuggle under the radiator in Angela's kitchen.

"Juliette is a person who likes order . . . like me," Poco told Georgina proudly. "Now that she's settled, she doesn't mind moving at all. We are very good and don't talk long at night. We know we need to get our beauty sleep."

"Beauty sleep. Good grief!" Georgina rolled a desperate eye. She wondered how she would ever get through an entire year of being friends with Poco without Angela there to help her.

Luckily, the problem would soon be partly solved. A new person was about to appear on the scene. He was not someone the friends had ever expected to know. Though he had been in their school classes for years, they had never spoken to him. He lived quite close to Poco, however, and this was why he happened to be walking by on the sidewalk when, with a terrible squeal of tires and a sickening thud, Juliette was run down by a car in the street.

Two

POCO RAN to the window the moment she heard the tires screech. Some flash of intuition told her what had happened. It was late afternoon. The big cat had just gone out. A bleary-eyed sun hung low in the sky.

"Juliette! Where are you?" Poco screamed. She saw a dark sports car speeding away. With another shriek of tires, it reached the end of the block, turned right, and disappeared.

Poco grabbed her coat and ran outside into the road. She searched the sidewalks up and down. An oddly shaped gray mound was lying near a street drain not far off.

"Oh no!" She crept toward it, hardly daring to

breathe. The mound became a tail bent, a head crushed, a body smashed on the cold pavement. Poco's stomach rose up. But when she stepped closer, the mound suddenly changed. It took on a brownish, brittle look, and she realized with a gasp that it was only a pile of leaves.

Poco stared weakly up the street. "Juliette? Please come. Are you hurt?"

Soft footsteps sounded behind her. A person wearing a baseball cap pulled far down over his eyes appeared at her side.

"If you are looking for your cat, it ran over there," the person said in a low voice. He pointed to a tangle of shrubs across the road and turned to leave.

"Wait!" Poco cried. "What happened? Did you see?"

The person turned back warily. He was a boy, short-legged and wiry, not much taller than Poco herself. There was something familiar about him, she thought.

"Your cat got hit," he said. "It flew up in the air like a football. I thought it came down on the Rollins' lawn, but it's not there now. Maybe it ran in the bushes."

"Which bushes?" Poco raced across the street.

The boy in the baseball cap followed and pointed. She pushed some branches aside, but there was nothing underneath.

"Maybe it kept running." The boy began to edge away again. Beneath his cap, his eyes surfaced and met hers, then drew back into shadow.

"Walter Kew!" Poco exclaimed. "I know who you are."

"Well, don't go yelling it around," Walter said, glancing over his shoulder. "I like to keep a low profile out here."

"A low what?" Poco tried to see his eyes again. They were the palest blue, very nearly white when the light shone in them.

"Never mind." Walter Kew pulled his cap down. "If I were you, I would look in the Rollins' backyard. The cat is probably hiding out there."

"Do you think she's hurt?" Poco said, gazing fearfully down the driveway. "Could you help me find her? My mother's at work. No one's home except me."

"Oh, all right," Walter muttered, but he didn't look happy about it.

The Rollins were berry people. Strawberries, blackberries, blueberries, raspberries—every sort of berry bush was planted in their yard. By this time of year, the berries were gone, leaving a snarl of brambles. Poco and Walter Kew waded in on tiptoes.

"Juliette! Please come out. Or make a noise and I'll find you," Poco coaxed.

"Cat? Here, cat," Walter Kew called.

There was no answer.

They walked back to the street and went around the block to the yard Juliette would have come to if she had kept going through the Rollins' brambles. Nothing was moving there, either.

Walter glanced over his shoulder. He grasped his baseball cap and pulled it farther down.

"I guess I'd better get going," he said. "I don't like being out on the street for too long."

"Why not?" Poco asked.

"Spirits," he said mysteriously. But then he stood around and didn't leave.

"You are Poco, right?" he said, looking at her sideways.

She nodded.

They inspected the second street up and down and asked some people on the sidewalk if they had seen a large gray Siamese cat. They hadn't.

There was no sign of Juliette. Poco began to feel sick again.

"Thanks for helping," she told Walter when they came back around to her house. "I guess I'll just sit on our porch steps for a while and see if she comes back."

"Time for me to disappear," he said. He slunk off down the sidewalk. About ten minutes later, though, Poco saw him coming back. He slipped into her yard like a spirit himself and scuttled up the path to the porch.

"I thought you might like some help waiting," he whispered, pulling up his cap a fraction of an inch. His pale eyes flashed out from under the brim. "I've had a few things disappear on me like that."

"Thanks." Poco moved to make room. "I guess the spirits are still watching you, right?"

"You never know," said Walter Kew. "It's a crazy world out there."

Poco called Georgina that night.

"Juliette was run over?" Georgina bellowed into the phone. "And now she's lost? I knew this would happen! It's Angela's fault for going away."

Poco held the receiver away from her ear.

"Are you sure Walter Kew was the person who came out and helped you?" Georgina went on shouting.

"Yes. He couldn't find her, either. But he said not to worry. He doesn't think Juliette is dead. Yet."

"How would Walter Kew know that? He never knows anything," Georgina pointed out. "He never speaks to anyone and he usually doesn't answer if someone speaks to him. His parents got killed when he was little, you know. Now he lives with his grandmother and is thought to be a strange person."

"I know," Poco said. "He is strange. But nice. He believes in spirits. He said we could use his Ouija board if we wanted, to find out where Juliette has gone. I said I'd let him know."

"Ouija board!"

"George, you don't have to yell every word you say," Poco said, holding the receiver out at arm's length. "My mother can hear you in the next room."

There was a rustling noise on Georgina's end of the line, as if she was changing position.

"Listen, Poco. Don't get mixed up with Walter Kew," she said in quieter but more earnest tones. "He has weird ideas. Anyway, Ouija boards are fake. Everybody knows it."

"I don't know it," Poco said stoutly.

"Yes, you do!" Georgina's voice rose again. "We used to do that stuff in second grade. It never told us anything we hadn't already figured out. Not only that but . . ."

Poco lay the phone down on the living room couch, where she was sitting, and got up and walked across the room. Georgina's voice went on without pause in the distance. It sounded like a flock of ducks quacking across a pond. After a while, Poco walked back and picked up the receiver again.

". . . *quack, quack, quack,* so I will come over to your house tomorrow, whether you like it or not, and help you look for Juliette," Georgina was saying. "She probably went under somebody's house. That's what cats always do—go under houses."

Poco hung up the phone completely when she heard this. She felt too worried to bother telling

Georgina that she was wrong, as usual. Cats do not "always do" anything. They are unpredictable, which is why humans, who are also unpredictable, love them so much. Furthermore, though a cat may go under a house, it usually will not stay there. This is because dust clogs up its sensitive nose and dirt falls onto its beautiful coat, and it is very shortly sneezing and miserable.

No, Juliette was not under a house at that moment. But in that case, where had she gone?

Poco took a telephone book out of a table drawer and looked up a number. She punched it into the telephone and waited through four rings.

"Hello! Speak up!" an elderly voice barked at the other end. Poco jumped. Old people made her nervous. They frequently looked angry or couldn't hear what she said.

"Hello?" she quavered. "May I speak to Walter Kew?"

Three

THE NEXT DAY at school Poco saw Walter Kew walking to his classroom. At least, she thought it was him whisking past in the shadows. Even in a bright-lit school corridor, he managed to make himself nearly invisible.

"Walter? Is that you?"

The figure stopped and glanced around. His baseball cap was pulled down so far that it looked as if the circulation was being cut off in his ears.

"I called you last night, remember?" Poco asked. "And you said . . ."

Walter placed a finger on his lips. With his head, he motioned her around a corner into an empty classroom. This was such weird behavior that Poco felt a small zing of alarm. But she followed him.

"For my Ouija board to operate, it needs privacy," Walter said when he had inspected the room to be sure it was vacant. "How are things at your house?"

"Things are fine," Poco said. "My mother works today so she won't be home until dinner. All my brothers are older and away at school."

"Good." Walter's eyes stared out from under his cap like two pale headlights. He looked twice as strange at school as he did outside.

"Would it be all right if my friend Georgina came, too?" Poco asked. "I already asked her actually, this morning before school. She doesn't completely believe in Ouija boards yet, but she said she'd try." This was a slight exaggeration. What Georgina had really said was, "I am not coming! No matter what! And don't you ever dare hang up on me again!"

"If she tries, your friend will believe," Walter said. "The Ouija works."

"Will it really be able to tell us where Juliette is?" Poco asked. "We're all so worried. My mother left some milk out on the porch last night, but Juliette never came."

"I can't guarantee anything," Walter said, "but this Ouija sees a lot. The board is old. It's got power to look into amazing places when you handle it right."

"I thought Ouija boards only tell you who you're going to marry or where you're going to live when you grow up," Poco said.

Walter Kew smiled. "That's what everyone thinks. A real Ouija is interested in real life, though. A lot of things go on around us all the time that we can't see. Bad stuff and good stuff. The Ouija finds it out. It sees and then it tells."

Poco was so excited by this report that she tried to run immediately to Georgina's classroom to tell her. Unfortunately the bell signaling the start of the school day rang at that moment, and she was forced to go back to her own room. This gave her time to think again, however. In the end, she decided not to pester Georgina anymore.

"George is like one of those old pack mules you see in the movies," Poco said to herself. "They take up a position in the middle of the road and refuse to budge no matter how hard you push or pull them. *But* if you go away and leave them alone, they get restless. Then, with no fuss at all, they end up walking in the very direction you wanted in the first place."

This, as it turned out, was exactly what happened. At three o'clock that afternoon, Georgina sauntered through the Lamberts' back door with a mulish air of indifference.

"So where is this great Ouija board?" she asked, gazing first at Poco and then at Walter Kew. They were sitting at the kitchen table with that very item between them, as Georgina could plainly see.

"Oh, hello, George. We were wondering when you'd get here," Poco said carelessly. But then, unable to contain her excitement, she jumped up. "Look at this Ouija board. Isn't it amazing? Have you met Walter Kew? He's amazing, too!"

○

WALTER KEW'S Ouija wasn't the ordinary kind—Georgina saw that in one glance. His board was made of wood, not the cardboard of the store-bought ones. The alphabet was painted across its glossy surface in two rows of dark red letters. Below the letters, the numerals one through ten were painted in blue. Odd symbols and designs filled the margins of the board.

Georgina walked across the kitchen and picked up the tear-shaped message wand that lay on the board. It was carved out of the same heavy wood. A clear circle of glass was embedded near the pointing end.

"This Ouija is from my family, way back in time," Walter Kew explained before Georgina could even ask. "My grandmother said it came across the ocean."

"Across the ocean!" Georgina looked at him suspiciously. "What ocean. From where?"

"I'm not sure. It's real, though. See that open eye?"

Poco nodded. In the upper left-hand corner of the board, a large lidless eye had been painted. It was dark in its interior and seemed to gaze straight at them.

"That's the Ouija's seeing eye," Walter said. "It can see anywhere you tell it to look."

"Anywhere?" Georgina asked. "You mean anywhere in the world?"

"I mean anywhere," Walter said, in such an ominous voice that an image of dark, unspeakable places leapt into Georgina's mind and she shivered.

"Poco, look! There's some sort of bird painted in the other corner," she said to cover her fright.

"It's a falcon," Poco replied. "You can tell by its curved beak and talons."

Walter Kew nodded at Poco. "That's right," he said. "It's a falcon that lived in the old-time countries. People used to hunt with them. Falcons caught rabbits and small animals. Their eyesight is very keen. That's why this one works for the Ouija."

"What do you mean?" Georgina asked. "What does it do?"

"It carries the Ouija eye high into the air and helps it to hunt for the places it must see into." Walter glanced down at the board again. "The other things you see painted here work for the Ouija, too. My grandmother told me about them. This is a sunbeam, for instance. . . ."

He pointed to a bright streak of yellow and orange in the lower right-hand corner of the board. "It gives the Ouija's eye light for looking into dark places. And this mountain goat is for walking up steep mountains and cliffs. That is a veil for showing when something is hidden behind something else. Here is a piece of rope, because you always end up needing rope wherever you go."

"Rope! Oh, come on!" Georgina gave a snort. There was something about this Ouija she didn't quite like.

"That's what my grandmother told me."

"And who is your grandmother?" Georgina folded her arms across her chest. "If you expect us to believe all this about the Ouija, you'd better start giving us a few more facts."

"George!" cried Poco, but it was too late. Walter Kew was already on his feet. He picked up the wonderful board and tucked it under his arm. Then he stuffed the wooden pointer into his jacket pocket.

"Oh, please!" Poco wailed. "You can't leave. We need to find Juliette before it's too late."

Walter looked angrily at Georgina. "The Ouija does not speak to people like her," he said. "It does not speak to people who try to insult it."

"Sorry!" said Georgina. "I didn't mean to insult anything. I just wanted to get a little background."

"Well, you used a very insulting voice," Walter Kew said. "If you want the Ouija to work, you will have to apologize to it."

"Apologize! To a Ouija board?" Georgina turned on him with battle-ready eyes. She was on the verge of opening her mouth to say a great deal more when Poco grabbed her and dragged her away into the living room.

"Georgina Rusk, if you don't apologize to Walter's Ouija board this minute, I will never speak to you again," Poco hissed. "And neither will Juliette, if we ever find her, which we never will if you keep on this way."

"Juliette never speaks to me, anyway," Georgina snapped, and stamped to the other side of the room. But after a moment, Poco saw that, for some reason, she had decided to give in. Perhaps, after all, Walter's board had impressed her.

"Oh, all right," she said, walking back toward the kitchen.

A minute later she had apologized to the Ouija's lidless eye and Walter Kew had settled into his chair. No sooner was he there than he placed his hands on the board and recited in a soft voice:

"Come together, all believers,
Let us turn this day to night
And surround the ancient Ouija
With the gloom it needs for sight."

Poco was enchanted. "Oh!" she breathed. "How do we do that?"

Georgina gave another of her loud, impatient snorts. "I suppose by pulling down the shades in this kitchen and turning out all the lights," she replied. "Is that right, Walter?"

He nodded, but kept his pale, spirit-seeing eyes well back under the brim of his cap. He and Georgina had taken a dislike to each other. If Poco had not sat between them, her tiny hands clenched together on her lap, there would have been no conversation with the Ouija that day.

"Please hurry," she said, gazing at Walter with trusting eyes. "Juliette is not very far away. She is waiting for us. I can feel it."

Four

If WALTER KEW had been strange and silent at school, now, in Poco's kitchen, he became another person. Under his baseball cap, his shy eyes flashed with authority, and even Georgina soon found herself taking orders from him. He was clearly practiced in the Ouija's peculiar ways. After the lights had been turned off and some curtains drawn as best they could be, he demanded that a single candle be lit and placed on the counter.

"Poco and I will work the wand," he announced, pushing his chair back from the table. He grasped the heavy Ouija board in both hands and settled it on his knees. Poco pulled her chair opposite his and took the board partway into her lap, sharing its weight.

"Georgina, you will ask the questions," Walter went on. "You must speak slowly so there is no mistake. Only one question at a time. And if you can't be serious, you'd better go home because the Ouija does not like to talk to silly persons."

"I will be serious," Georgina said in such an obedient voice that Poco looked up in surprise.

"I usually start by asking some warm-up questions before the real ones," Walter explained. "Then the Ouija has time to get its search system working. Watch the wand after that. It always tells the truth. It's told me things about my family in the past, things I needed to know that no one else would tell me. Also, I've contacted people on it."

"Who?" Poco asked.

Walter looked down. "I don't think I should say."

"Why not?" Georgina demanded.

He shifted uneasily in his seat. "Well, all right, if you promise to keep it secret."

"Of course we will," Georgina said.

Walter Kew leaned toward them. "I've spoken

to my parents," he whispered. "They were killed when I was a baby."

Neither Poco nor Georgina could think of what to say. Everyone in school knew that Walter Kew's parents had been killed years ago. It was one of those dreadful facts that nobody ever mentioned. Now, the thought of Walter talking to his dead parents' spirits made the friends glance around nervously.

"Well, that's great you got through to them," Poco finally managed to say. "They must've been really glad to hear from you!"

Walter nodded.

"How were they killed, anyway?" Georgina asked. "No one ever seemed to know."

Walter sighed. "I don't know, either," he said. "I was too little to remember, and my grandparents would never tell me. I guess it was so awful they didn't want to think about it. But I can't help wondering. That's why I got the Ouija to help. Do you know that I've never even seen a photograph of my parents?"

Georgina and Poco were astounded. "But why?" "Every family has pictures." "What happened to yours?"

"I don't know." Walter shrugged. "They just disappeared, I guess. My grandmother told me they must have gotten lost."

This was such a strange thing to have happened that the friends hardly knew what to think. They were about to ask Walter more when he reached up and pulled his cap down hard over his eyes. It was as if a curtain had dropped on a stage. Georgina and Poco knew not to say another word.

"Come on, let's get this Ouija working," Walter said from under his cap. "No more wasting time. The first thing we do is have sixty seconds of quiet. That's to clear the airways. Then Georgina can begin asking questions. Do you have a watch? Okay, are we ready?"

Everyone nodded.

Walter placed his fingertips lightly on the edge of the wand. Poco did the same, in the traditional way. A deep silence came down over the room while the single candle flickered and shadows leapt on the walls. Slowly even the outside noises from the street seemed to fade, and a new, exotic air entered the space around their chairs. It was an air so different from the one in the kitchen before that Poco was nearly sure an unknown force had arrived. She thought of Walter's parents. Had they come to watch? Looking across at Walter, she wondered how it would be to have two such powerful spirits hovering over one's everyday life.

"The first question is . . . !" Georgina's voice rang out rather sooner than expected. Patience was certainly not her strong point. "The first question is, What is Angela doing in Mexico right this minute?"

This was a respectable start. Under Poco's fingertips, the wand sprang to life and went to perch on the sharp-eyed falcon. A moment later, it slid to the right and paused over the dark red *S*, then moved left until the letter *L* showed through its glass eye. Next it inched up toward the beginning of the alphabet and sat atop the letter *E* for what seemed like a long time. With a lurch, it headed toward the *M*, passed over it, and went on to pause at the *P*. Next it visited, in quick succession, the *I*, *N*, and *G*, and drifted off. It returned to the falcon and halted.

Walter Kew lifted his fingers off the wand and looked up.

"Did you understand the answer?" he asked. "It was pretty clear."

Poco looked confused. "I know it started with the *S*, and then went to the *L* and *E*, and finally the *P*," she said, "but I couldn't tell what it was spelling. The last part was *I-N-G*, I think. I suppose Angela must be do-*ING* something. But what?"

Walter smiled. "Not bad," he said. "The trick was the *E*. The wand stayed over it for a long time, which means it was double.

"I still don't get it," Poco said. Beside her, Georgina snapped her fingers.

"I do!" she cried. "The answer is *SLEEPING*. That's what Angela's doing right now."

"Sleeping!" said Poco. "Why would Angela be sleeping in the middle of the day. Is she sick?"

Walter Kew pushed his baseball cap back on his head. "I don't think so," he said. "I couldn't figure it out, either, for a second. Mexico is a couple of hours behind us in time, so it must be about two o'clock in the afternoon there. Then I remembered: in Mexico, it's hot in the middle of the day, even in winter. So people take siestas after lunch. You know, naps."

"Angela is taking a nap?" Poco exclaimed. "But that's terrible! I imagined her doing exciting things down there, like learning Spanish or hunting for vampires."

"Well, I suppose she can't always be doing exciting things just because she's in Mexico," Walter said. "In fact, I suppose life down there isn't all that different from life up here. It has its adventures, and then it has its naps."

This was such an obvious point that Poco felt ridiculous. She looked at Walter with even more respect.

Georgina was tapping her foot and gazing at the ceiling, though. She wanted to go on.

"Question number two!" she announced. Poco and Walter put their fingers back quickly on the wand.

"What is Miss Bone doing at Angela's house right now?" Georgina intoned.

This was a rather boring question, but Poco leaned forward and waited for the answer to begin. "Knitting," she imagined the board replying. Or "writing letters." Maybe the Ouija was bored, too. The wand didn't move.

"Who is this person, Miss Bone?" Walter asked when another motionless minute had dragged by.

"She's the old lady the Harralls hired to live

in their garage apartment. To look after their house," Poco explained. "I guess she's not home now or something."

"Ask the question again," Walter said.

Georgina cleared her throat. "What is Miss Bone, the woman who is living at Angela Harrall's house, doing right now?" she said slowly.

The wand wobbled after this, but then its energy seemed to drain away and it sat still again. After about a minute, it began an awkward crab-like creep toward the board's bottom edge, where it would have fallen off if Walter hadn't stopped it.

"That's strange," he said. "The Ouija has never done that before." He picked up the wand and looked at it. "There's been some mix-up, probably. Let's not worry about it. Just go ahead and ask about Juliette. We're beginning to run out of time."

"Here we go, then," Georgina said, and, with a little shiver of expectation, she asked in a loud voice,

"Oh, wonderful Ouija, please tell us where Juliette is hiding! Find Juliette now with your magic eye so we can bring her home tonight!"

There was another period of stillness. For a

while, it seemed that the Ouija might have forgotten them completely and gone off on some cosmic errand. But then, with a burst, the wand came to life.

It moved first to the bright sunbeam in the corner, then slipped down to linger over the wide, elegant *H* at the board's center. From there it slid left and covered the *O*, backed around and visited the *M*. It zipped up again and over to the *E*. After this, it went back to the sunbeam in the corner, perhaps to rest itself in that figure's rosy glow. There seemed to be nothing further coming, so Walter Kew raised his fingers from the wand and looked up.

"*H-O-M-E*," Poco said. "Home. Does that mean Juliette has already come back? Is she somewhere around here?"

"It could be," Walter said.

Poco sprang to her feet. "I'm going to look."

"Me, too!" Georgina cried.

They put on their coats and tore out into the yard. There, for the next ten minutes, they searched high and low—under bushes and up trees, around the front yard and on the porch roof. Nowhere did they see anything resembling a gray Siamese cat. They were thinking of going back inside when Walter came out with his coat on. He was carrying the Ouija in a box under his arm.

"Are you sure the Ouija was telling us the truth?" Georgina called to him across the yard. "We can't find Juliette anywhere!"

Walter didn't answer. He walked up the driveway toward the sidewalk out front.

"Wait!" Georgina shouted. She caught him as he was about to slink through the Lamberts' front gate. No sooner had he come outside than his old nervous habits had returned. Even as he walked, he was pulling down his baseball cap, glancing fearfully over his shoulder.

"Walter Kew! Has this all been some kind of trick?" Georgina demanded with hard eyes.

"Of course not." He kept walking.

"Well, what should we do now?" she asked, jogging along beside him. "Poco is very upset. She was depending on the Ouija to find Juliette."

They both glanced back at Poco's tiny figure rushing frantically around the yard. She couldn't believe the old cat wasn't there.

"Has Poco thought that the Ouija might have meant something else?" Walter asked Georgina.

"*What* else?"

Walter shrugged. "Home is where you start from, not where you happen to be," he said. Before Georgina could ask him anything else, his short, wiry legs shot out, and he disappeared up the sidewalk.

Five

"WHAT A STRANGE thing to say," Poco exclaimed when Georgina reported Walter's parting words. "He really is the oddest person. It must come from having only a grandmother in his family instead of a mother and father and aunts and uncles like everybody else."

"And not having any photographs to see what they looked like," Georgina said. "It's so queer. I would begin to wonder if I was who people said I was. Maybe that's why he wants to make contact with his parents. Do you think he really talks to them? Or does he just pretend, to make himself feel better?"

Poco frowned at her friend. "If Walter Kew says he's talked to his parents, then he has," she declared. "Really, George, you are the most suspicious person. I know tiny field mice who have more trust in the world than you. Don't you know that there are times you just have to believe, because it's the only way."

"I have never *had* to believe in anything," Georgina sniffed. "And I don't plan to start. What I believe in is sticking to the facts."

"Well, if Walter is right, we can be sure of one fact," Poco said. "Juliette is probably walking around in Angela's yard at this very moment. Come on! Let's go look."

The winter afternoon was coming to an end as the two set off at top speed along the sidewalk toward the Harralls' house. They were not even halfway there when the sun plunged below the horizon. Cars passing in the road began to turn on their headlights. Poco didn't notice. She trotted along the street on her elf-tiny feet. Georgina trailed behind, showing rather less energy.

"Couldn't we get up early tomorrow and look for Juliette then?" she called out. "It'll be too dark to see anything when we get there." The air had grown so cold that her words came out in white clouds.

"It doesn't matter," Poco called back. "We can hear. And smell!"

"Smell!" Georgina snorted. There were times when Poco made a person wonder if she wasn't, with all her animal connections, turning into some small furry beast herself. A prairie dog, maybe. They had the same cute eyes and snub noses.

"What I mean is, smell the catnip," Poco shouted over her shoulder without slowing down. "It grows in certain places in the Harralls' yard. Juliette loves it. She told me once that for cats catnip is strong medicine, with power to cure sickness and wounds. I bet that's where we'll find her. If we can't see her, we'll sniff her out."

Georgina did not know how to reply to this ridiculous idea without hurting Poco's feelings, so she kept quiet. Luckily, they soon arrived at the Harralls' front walk. But then—oh, dear!— one look made Georgina want to run in the opposite direction.

Never had a place looked so forbidding. While all the other houses on the street glowed with friendly lights, Angela's house sat dark as a hunk of coal in its yard. The windows were black; the porches lurked in shadow; the chimneys rose against the sky like a devilish pair of horns. The yard was already largely invisible, though night had not yet fully fallen.

"What do we do now?" Georgina whispered.

"We walk around and look. And call." Poco spoke calmly, but even she felt nervous. "If we stay together, we'll be all right," she instructed Georgina, who was now plainly cowering at her side.

"I don't like this!"

"Come on, George. You're being silly."

"It's too dark."

"Hold my hand. . . . Juliette! Here, Juliette!"

"I don't think she's here."

"Juliette! Please come out." Poco strode about the yard, dragging Georgina behind her.

"Poco, look. There are lights over there."

"That's just the garage apartment where Miss Bone is staying. Georgina! What is wrong with you. You're shaking!"

"I'm freezing! I'm going home."

"Well, all right. Maybe Juliette hasn't gotten here yet. But let's go knock on Miss Bone's door first. She might have seen something. She's home, I think. I just saw a shadow at the window."

Suddenly Georgina gasped. "Poco! Look!"

They had made their way around the house by this time and were standing just opposite the three enormous garage doors. The Harralls, having plenty of money, always did things in a larger-than-life sort of way, and their garage was no exception. It was as big as most people's houses, with an apartment up on the second floor. The entrance was a small door to one side. Because night had come, the door was now lit by an overhead lamp. There, on the raised stone stoop below the door, a row of strange little bodies was arranged.

"What are they?" Poco cried.

Georgina inched closer and peered down. "I don't know. Mice?"

Poco came forward into the light and looked for herself.

"Three moles and two field mice. All dead," she reported in a hollow tone. "What are they doing here? And lined up in this terrible way?"

As if in answer, the loud click of a door opening above came to their ears, followed by the sound of heavy footsteps descending an interior staircase.

Poco turned wide eyes on Georgina. "It's Miss Bone!" she hissed. "Quick! Let's hide!"

For reasons they could not have explained, the friends fled out of the light and across the driveway toward the Harralls' house. Some large bushes rose in their path. They slid behind them. Only just in time!

The outside door to the garage apartment opened, and a tall, gray-haired woman stepped into the light. She peered suspiciously into the darkness, then raised a rather beaky nose into the air and sniffed.

Snuff. Her face turned toward the street.

Snuff. Her head came around and seemed to scan the driveway up and down.

Snuff. All of a sudden, as if she had homed in on their scent, Miss Bone looked exactly in the friends' direction. Behind their bushes, Poco and Georgina stood paralyzed with fear.

Soon, however, Miss Bone's nose dropped toward the gruesome little assemblage at her feet. Bending down, she examined the bodies. She turned two of them over with a long pointed finger.

After another most peculiar-sounding snuff ("I've heard anteaters make a noise like that," Poco told Georgina later), she gathered the moles and mice together in her hands and turned and went back inside. The door closed behind her. The tread of her feet could be heard returning up the stairs. The inside door opened . . . and shut with its distinctive click.

A full minute passed before the bushes moved on the far side of the Harralls' driveway. Then two shadowy forms slunk forth. They slid noise-lessly onto the grass, darted around the back of the house, and went up toward the street. There, after a short, breathless conference, they melted into the night, each running in a different direc-tion down the sidewalk—toward home.

○

NOT UNTIL the next afternoon, when they met after lunch in the school library, did Poco and Georgina speak about what they had seen at Angela's house. By then, they'd had the long night to think it over. Poco, especially, looked pale around the gills. She had been invaded by a desperate feeling that she would never see Juliette again.

"Georgina! What shall we do? Something is going on at Angela's house. I'm sure of it!"

"I think we shouldn't get upset yet," Georgina replied. "Last night was weird, all right. But it could be explained."

"You always say that!" Poco exploded. "But there is something horrible about that woman, Miss Bone. I've felt it since she first moved in. Remember when I told you that Angela's yard had changed?"

"Hmmm." Georgina kept watch over Poco's shoulder, in case anyone should come into the library. Their conversation sounded odd in that sensible, bookish place.

"I thought it was just winter," Poco went on. "You know, all the little animals hiding away and the birds flying south. But now I think something else may be happening."

"You don't believe that Miss Bone killed those animals!" Georgina looked at her friend in horror. "She's just an old teacher—you said it yourself."

"Well, someone killed them. Maybe someone who's in her power."

"In her power! Who?"

"Well . . . Juliette? It's been two days since she

ran off. My mother is making posters. We're going to drive around town this afternoon and put them up. Also"—Poco glanced at Georgina— "my mother is going to speak to Miss Bone."

"You mean, ask her if she's seen Juliette?"

"Right."

"Oh, well, that should settle it," Georgina said. She heaved a sigh of relief. "I was beginning to think that we scared ourselves about nothing, anyway. What did we really see? A bunch of animals that probably died of cold, for that matter. Miss Bone was as surprised to find them as we were."

"She was not!"

Georgina folded her arms. "Listen, Poco. You're imagining things. If Miss Bone says she's seen Juliette, we'll just go back and find her. In the daylight this time."

"And if Miss Bone says she hasn't seen Juliette?"

"Well, I don't know. What?"

"Then we'll ask Walter Kew if we can use his board again," Poco said, her voice falling to a whisper. "Because she might be lying. The board will tell us the truth."

"I don't know why you trust that board," Georgina said irritably. "I think it's completely unreliable. Remember how it broke down and couldn't answer my question about—"

Poco grabbed Georgina's arm to stop her. "Ssh!" She glanced over her shoulder, looking so much like Walter that Georgina felt a jab of alarm. "Your question was about Miss Bone," Poco hissed. "Remember, George? Can you see how there's beginning to be a pattern?"

"Good grief! If there's going to be that kind of pattern, I don't want to think about it."

"I'm sorry, but you have to think about it," Poco said sternly, "because Juliette's life may be at stake."

"Juliette's life!" Georgina didn't know what to say. Poco was leaping to the blackest sorts of conclusions.

"We will see what we will see," Poco continued. "I'll call you at home this afternoon, as soon as I hear what my mother finds out."

Georgina nodded. She felt totally confused. A sudden wild desire to see Angela surged up inside her. Angela had never seemed especially remarkable before. She had seemed, if anything, rather stubborn and thin-skinned. But now, without her, Georgina could see that the group was somehow losing its balance. They were like a cart rushing headlong downhill on two wheels.

"Oh, Angela, if you would just come back!" Georgina cried under her breath as she watched Poco's determined little prairie-dog shape trot away along the school corridor. "We are all lost without you. Not just Juliette."

Six

GEORGINA DID NOT wait at home very long for Poco's telephone call that afternoon. She was far too impatient for that. Hardly had she come in—rather late after a Girl Scout meeting—when she dropped her book bag on the floor, wrote a note to her mother (who was herself at the supermarket), and left in a rush for the Lamberts' house.

"Hello, Georgina. Poco is not here," Mrs. Lambert said, opening the back door. "She's gone to Walter Kew's house to do something. We have just spent two hours putting up lost cat notices. No one has seen Juliette anywhere! Not even nice old Miss Bone at the Harralls' house." (Georgina's eyes shifted slightly at this.) "What on earth can we tell Angela when she calls next time?"

Georgina shrugged. "Tell her that Juliette was so furious to be left behind that she decided to become an invisible and live with the fairies. Angela believes in that sort of thing, and who knows? Juliette was always a mysterious cat."

"How I wish it could be true," Mrs. Lambert said, rubbing her temples. "It's supposed to snow tonight. Poor, poor Juliette. I'm afraid we may have seen the last of the old dear."

Walter Kew lived down the street and around the corner from the Lamberts. Georgina set out right away. The house was small and overgrown with vines. A cockeyed sign nailed to the fence out front said HOME OF FRED B. DOCKER. PASS YE WHO DARE. This referred to Walter's grandfather, a kind but blustery grocery store owner who had passed into final realms himself several years before. Walter wasn't exaggerating about the shrunken state of his family.

Georgina pounded on the shabby front door. She rang the doorbell three times in a row.

"Coming!" a voice croaked from inside. The door was opened by an old woman with a cane.

"I suppose you want my grandson?" she demanded. "He is up in his room with another visitor. Would you care to wait, or join them?"

"Join them, please!"

"Go on up, then. Second door on the left. Walter is very popular today," his grandmother added, thrusting her head forward and blinking like a curious old sea turtle. "Company, company, left, right, and center!"

Georgina fled up the stairs. Old people were so unsettling. They were always peering and probing, as if children had some secret they would like to get at.

Poco and Walter were in the midst of pulling down the shades in his room and preparing the Ouija board.

"So! Here you are, you double-crossing rats!" Georgina cried, charging through the door. "Poco, you were supposed to call me and—"

One look at Poco's face brought her to a halt. It was red, and puffy around the eyes.

"Oh no! What's the matter?"

Walter stepped forward protectively. "She's worried," he said. "Her mother told her that Juliette is most likely . . . um . . ."

"Dead!" wailed Poco. She hid her face in her hands.

"Oh, Poco! Don't cry. We'll find her. I know we will!" Georgina couldn't bear to see her in tears. Poco never cried.

"She was my friend," Poco said in a trembling voice. "She slept at the end of my bed every night. We loved each other."

"I told Poco we'd ask the Ouija to find out about Juliette once and for all," Walter said. "Poco can't wait anymore. She has to know the truth!"

He looked quite upset himself and kept yanking his baseball cap up and down over his eyes. "Since you're here, could you ask the questions again?" he asked Georgina. "Poco wants to work the wand with me."

Georgina nodded unhappily. She wished Poco had not come here. In the end, she would be disappointed, the way she had been before. Or worse, she would be hurt. Georgina saw her staring grimly at the Ouija's glistening letters, as if they were her very last hope in the world.

Walter was already lighting the single candle, however. He rested the board on Poco's knees and recited the odd little chant:

"Come together, all believers,
Let us turn this day to night

And surround the ancient Ouija
With the gloom it needs for sight."

With a swiftness that Georgina found hardly possible, the air in the room changed. It became private air, secret air, air that pushed back the real world all around so that a space was opened for the Ouija's lidless eye. Was it really magic? Georgina felt the skin prickle on the back of her neck. She glanced at Walter, but his eyes were hidden under his cap. Outside, the noises of the neighborhood began to fade. . . .

If this was real magic, Georgina knew suddenly that it was not a good kind. There was something disturbing about that eye. It was so dark and unblinking. So strong. Too strong, she thought, to be used for lost cats.

"Couldn't we just go outside and try looking for Juliette by ourselves?" she begged the others. "I'm sure if we went to Angela's house again, we really might—"

"No!" Poco interrupted before she could even finish. Walter also was shaking his head. "Remember when I said sometimes you have to believe?" Poco asked her. "Please try to now, because it's the only way."

EVEN BEFORE the questions started, it was
clear that this meeting with the Ouija would
be different from the one before. The darkness
seemed darker, the candle burned brighter, and
the three in the room felt farther away from the
real world beyond the windows.

Walter was on edge. He barked out his com-
mands and took a great deal of trouble arrang-
ing them around the board. By the time he and
Poco placed their fingers on the wand, there was
so much tension that plain breathing had become difficult.

Into this thick atmosphere, Georgina flung
her opening question, a warm-up one about
when the first snow of that winter would fall.
Without hesitation, the Ouija spelled out *T-O-
N-I-G-H-T*, a reasonable answer since the sky
was clouded and weather forecasters everywhere had been predicting snow since early
morning.

"Good," Walter Kew said. "We're on the right
track."

Georgina's second question (another warm-
up) asked for the color of Juliette's eyes. She'd

had the bright idea to start the Ouija thinking about the old cat.

A-Z-U-R-E, the answer came back, making everyone think the board had sneezed, or was perhaps "unsure" of how to spell. Then Walter remembered that azure was a shade of blue. Exactly which shade he couldn't recall. It didn't seem to matter. Juliette's beautiful Siamese eyes were blue.

Finally, while Poco's face alternated between steamed-up red and ghostly white, Georgina inquired about the cat herself.

"Dear, kind Ouija, please tell us what yard Juliette is hiding in so we can find her," she begged. "Tell us if she has been taken inside or is being held prisoner. If Juliette is lying in the bushes along a road, please give us the name of the road. If she is under a house"—Georgina felt, rather than saw, Poco's frown—"let us know whose and where. Also, is she hurt? Also—"

"Stop," Walter Kew murmured. "That's enough. The wand has started to move."

Like a ship drifted off its mooring, the wand began to float over the glossy surface of the board. Aimlessly it wandered hither and yon, pausing in places where there was no meaning to be had, moving on again.

A minute later, though, it picked up speed. It swept toward Poco's edge of the board, then toward Walter's. It pirouetted on the Ouija's great eye, then sped headlong into the mass of red letters. It halted over one. Georgina leaned forward to look through the glass circle.

"D," she announced. The message had begun! Other letters came rapidly.

"E," Georgina said. "A." And, after a scuffle, "D" again.

Poco's eyes widened into terrified saucers at this, and she toppled back on the bed where she had been sitting. "I knew it!" she wailed, and would have given up there and then if Walter had not shouted at her to put her fingers back on the wand.

"It's still moving! It has something else to say!"

So Poco got into position again, though tears were streaming down her cheeks. Soon the wand stopped over another letter.

"L," whispered Georgina.

Ten seconds later came "Y." After this, the wand rushed to the painted veil and sat still upon it for at least half a minute.

The wand started up again.

"Good grief!" Georgina said. "Is there even more?

"*E,*" she cried out. And then, during a mad series of dashes and halts: "*N.*" "*E.*" "*M.*" "*Y.*"

Afterward, a tremendous shiver arose from the board. It passed through the wand up Poco's and Walter's arms. Poco let out a shriek and fell back again on the bed.

"What was that!" she gasped. "Oh, it was awful!"

Walter Kew was frightened as well. He snatched his fingers from the wand as if they had received a shock.

Georgina, standing over them, was the most startled of all. She had not felt the Ouija tremble, but she was the first to understand its message.

"Deadly enemy!" she whispered. Poco and Walter stared up at her.

"We have a deadly enemy," she said again. "That's the Ouija's message."

Poco sat up suddenly. She removed the wand from the board and took the board from her knees. She placed them carefully on Walter's bed. Her face was calm. Her eyes were clear. It was as if she'd received the very news she'd expected and no longer had to worry about what was coming.

"Deadly enemy," she repeated. "I'm so glad to know it for sure. I thought there must be someone at the bottom of this. Whoever they are and wherever they may be, there can be no question now what has happened to Juliette!"

Seven

WHEN HAD A Ouija board ever solved so many mysteries so fast? For the first time in days, Poco felt happy. Not only was she sure that the deadly enemy had kidnapped Juliette, she also knew who the deadly enemy was! Everything pointed to it—her worries and fears about Juliette's disappearance, her suspicions about Angela's yard and the old woman who had moved into the apartment above the garage.

Miss Bone. There could be no other.

Georgina looked frightened when Poco explained the facts to her and Walter Kew during lunch the next day. Unfortunately the Ouija's predicted snowstorm had amounted to only a fine dusting. They were all sitting as usual in the school's dreary basement cafeteria.

"Miss Bone!" Georgina cried. "Oh, Poco! Do you really think so?"

"I'm positive. I have good antennae about these things. I would have told you yesterday, but I didn't want to upset you any more than you already were."

"I must have terrible antennae," Georgina replied. "Angela's yard looked fine to me. I wouldn't have thought anything was wrong there if you hadn't told me."

"What *is* wrong there?" asked Walter, who was huddled at their lunch table, trying to look as invisible as possible. Georgina couldn't help glaring at him. She was not at all resigned to having him in their group. He was a strange person. Also, he seemed to be slouching unnecessarily close to Poco.

"The yard was invaded by an evil power just after the Harralls went to Mexico," Poco explained to him. "The little animals who lived there began to disappear. We aren't sure whether they were scared away or whether something bad has been happening to them."

There was a pause while Walter pulled his

baseball cap up just high enough to fit a sandwich underneath. Georgina took a bite of her hot lunch. Poco was too nervous to eat.

"You should try drinking a little milk at least," Walter said, looking concerned. "Even when you're worried, you have to keep up your strength."

Poco shook her head and pushed her lunch aside. "One thing we figured out is that Miss Bone collects the bodies of small animals," she went on. "Mice and moles. We saw her pick them up ourselves."

"What does she do with them?" Walter asked.

"We don't know," Georgina said.

"Yet," added Poco. "You can see why George and I are so worried about Juliette. If she went back 'home,' as the Ouija board told us she did, she would have run directly into Miss Bone."

"But didn't Miss Bone tell your mother she hadn't seen Juliette?" Walter asked.

Poco exhaled sharply. "Miss Bone wouldn't tell on herself, would she? If a person has an uncontrollable appetite for small animals, she would never admit it!"

"An uncontrollable appetite! Oh, how horrible!" Georgina exclaimed. She pushed her hot lunch away and covered it with several layers of paper napkins. "Do you think that's what Miss Bone has been doing? Eating those poor little animals?"

"There is no way to know what she does with them," Poco replied briskly, "without a more thorough investigation. I know we promised Angela not to start anything until she got back. But I think in this case even she would want it. Her house is in the clutches of an unknown power. Also, Juliette's life may depend on what we find."

"If Juliette still has a life," Walter Kew cautioned. "She could be a Siamese spirit by now." He gazed sadly at Poco, and it was clear he saw some likeness in their situations. Slowly he was losing his awkwardness around her, and even around Georgina. Not that he acted any less strange elsewhere. He still hid in the shadows of the school corridors and refused to speak to people. In fact, it was quite daring of Poco and Georgina to be seen here sitting with him at lunch. He had never been invited to join any group before.

"Walter, that is not a nice thing to say," Poco told him severely. "You are much too concerned with spirits. I am beginning to think you are more interested in the dead than you are in the living."

"I am," Walter admitted. "They are easier to talk to."

Georgina cast her eyes upward. "Our group is operating under the belief that Juliette is alive and well and can be rescued," she said. "If you can't believe that, you can't be with us."

"No problem. I believe it," Walter said. "What should we do next? Ask the Ouija about Miss Bone?"

"That," replied Georgina, "is the one thing we are *not* going to do. We've had enough of that weird Ouija eye. I am beginning to think it may be dangerous!"

At this moment, a bell rang. Everyone in the lunchroom leapt to their feet and made for the trash barrels with trays and bags.

"Come over to my house after school," Georgina told the others under cover of the scuffle. "What we need to do now is set up a system for investigating Miss Bone."

"You mean for spying on her?" Walter inquired, holding the door open for Poco.

"Yes," Georgina snapped. "That's exactly what I mean."

GEORGINA'S spy system was amazingly easy to arrange. It consisted mostly of two or more members of the group hiding, whenever possible, in the bushes across from Miss Bone's garage apartment. These were the same bushes that the friends had fled to on that first frightening night. They proved especially useful now because they could be reached from behind the Harralls' main house. Miss Bone could not see the investigators going in or coming out.

Not that she would have seen anyone, anyway. Sight, it soon appeared, was not Miss Bone's most powerful sense. This was discovered by Poco and Walter when they saw her smash her car into the Harralls' garage door one evening as she was returning home.

"Miss Bone couldn't see that the garage door was down," Poco reported to the group the next day. "She thought it was up and tried to drive through."

"It *is* painted black," Walter said. "And she didn't have her headlights on, because it wasn't quite dark."

"Remember how Miss Bone tried to sniff us out the first time we watched her?" Georgina asked Poco. "I think her nose is sharper than her eyes, and that she picks up information that way, sort of like a . . ."

"Shark," Poco said.

"Yes!"

"Or a bat. Vampire bats smell blood close to the surface of the skin."

Georgina glanced around nervously at this, but since they were only in Poco's kitchen eating popcorn after school, there did not seem much chance of such creatures being nearby.

"Anything else to report?" she asked the investigators.

"Miss Bone is very old and very ugly," Poco said. "She has crooked teeth and a wart on her chin."

"She has enormous hands with blue veins all over their backs," Walter added. "And pointed feet. There is a lump where her shoulders meet."

"Yes, I've noticed that. It gives her a weird bend. What is it?"

No one knew.

She wore a long, rough, wheat-colored cape, a type of clothing the group had never seen on anyone before.

"It reminds me of something from the olden days," Georgina said.

"It reminds me of witches," Poco said straight out, a thought they'd all begun to have. "Any normal old woman would go to the hairdresser and have her hair done right. Even Walter's grandmother goes and gets a permanent. Miss Bone's hair scraggles around as if she doesn't care."

"Maybe she has more important things to think about," Walter said.

"That's what I'm afraid of," Poco replied.

Daily they watched Miss Bone for signs that Juliette was in her power. And nightly they came also, when they could find an excuse to get out of the house. Walter had the easiest time because his grandmother went to bed early, or at least turned off her hearing aid so that he could sneak past her in the kitchen. He became the usual night watchman at the Harralls' garage, a position he liked so well that he didn't mind going outside anymore and stopped his dreadful slinking walk—at least after six P.M.

Poco took the afternoons with Georgina, when one or the other didn't have to go to Girl Scouts or piano lessons. And Georgina took the weekends with Walter because Poco so often had to visit relatives or have them in to visit her. The Lambert clan was togetherish, as Georgina frequently complained.

"You should tell your family that you are a person with a life of your own!" she advised Poco. "How can they expect you to grow up and get anything done in the world when you're constantly having to go to all their lunches and dinners?"

For the most part, everyone came to watch whenever they could. The weather was mild for early December. No other snowstorms threatened. There were many afternoons when the bushes across from Miss Bone's door hid all three investigators at once and could be seen to shake from the bottled-up energy and whispering going on behind them.

Miss Bone not only looked strange, she had many disturbing habits, the investigation soon revealed. She liked being out after dark. With a small but powerful flashlight, she prowled the neighborhood, often stopping on the sidewalk to peer into other people's lighted windows.

She was attracted to the moon and sometimes came outside simply to stand in its cold glare.

She collected mysterious plants and grasses from along the roadsides, and brought them back to her apartment. She also collected mushrooms, strange spiked flowers, and bird nests, which she set out to dry on the little front stoop. (Georgina inspected this place, close up, whenever she dared.)

Poco, driving home with her mother one day, passed Miss Bone's dark, rusty car parked by the road and, looking beyond it to a field, saw her caped figure holding a butterfly net, ready to strike.

Walter watched her come into a hardware store where he and his grandmother had gone to buy a snow shovel. He followed her to the counter and heard her ask the store man for rat poison.

"Rat poison!" Poco's and Georgina's eyes opened wide when they heard this.

Walter nodded. "And the store man said, 'What, Miss Bone? Back for more already?' "

"Good grief!" cried Georgina. "Maybe she has been poisoning all those little animals."

Walter looked worriedly at Poco to see how she would take this, for if Miss Bone had been poisoning moles and mice, might she not also have done it to Juliette?

"I will not think of such things," Poco said, turning her head away. "Until we have evidence. We must keep up our investigation. Harder than ever!"

Eight

THE MOST SUSPICIOUS thing of all about Miss Bone was that she lived alone. She had never had a husband, never had a child; she had never had anyone that Poco's mother, or Georgina's, could think of. It made a person wonder what had gone wrong.

"I guess she was just an English teacher, forever and ever," Mrs. Lambert said. "Then she retired."

"How about brothers and sisters? Or parents?" Poco asked while Georgina and Walter stood nearby listening. Not wanting to leave any stone unturned, the investigators had begun to interview likely informants. "Whoever you're related to, it shows who you are," Walter had advised them.

"Miss Bone's family? Oh, I wouldn't know that!" Mrs. Lambert protested. "She is so much older. Nearly seventy, I think. The school let her stay on a few extra years."

"Miss Bone with a boyfriend!" Georgina's mother smiled when they asked her. "Not that I know of, but who am I to say? I've never been near enough to her even to shake hands."

None of the investigators had been near Miss Bone, either—that was the trouble. They hadn't noticed her before she came to Angela's, and now, after the Ouija's dreadful message, they were too frightened to get close. They watched her from a distance and were careful to keep well away if she appeared in places where they were. Such long-range observation could not go on forever, though. Inevitably the moment must come when they would have to move in to gather more information.

It happened before anyone was ready, on a cold Tuesday afternoon in early December. Poco was the only watchman on duty that day. She stood shivering in the bushes across from the Harralls' garage and was beginning to think of going home to get warm when Miss Bone stepped out her apartment door. She was wearing her cape and an elegant fur hat whose soft gray color reminded Poco distinctly of . . . !

"Oh no! Juliette!" But that was beyond imagination. Poco closed her eyes and shook her head fiercely.

When she opened them again, Miss Bone was switching on the outside overhead light. Then she closed the door (but did not lock it), walked to the garage, and tried to start her car. The motor was cold and took a long time to get going. When it had caught, she backed out of the garage with a truly evil expression on her face and drove away.

Poco, who had watched this kind of departure many times, stepped out of the bushes into a weak patch of sun. Usually when the investigators were left alone this way, they amused themselves by peeping in the windows of Angela's house or sneaking around the big yard looking for clues. Now, whether from cold or the sight of Miss Bone's fur hat or just the terrible weariness of worrying about Juliette, Poco decided on a more drastic form of action. She crossed the driveway, stepped up on the stone stoop, pulled open the apartment door, and entered.

The stairs were before her, and she walked up. At the top, a landing was lit by another overhead light that Miss Bone had turned on to welcome her home. Poco tried the inside door to her apartment. It was open! With a fluttering heart, she went in.

The kitchen was small but tidy. Several old-fashioned aprons hung on hooks behind the door. The only table was covered by a lace table-cloth, yellowed with age. China jars that read *Tea*, *Sugar*, and *Flour* in antique script sat upon the counter, along with a blackened teakettle. There was a basket filled with dried flowers. Or were they herbs and grasses?

Poco leaned forward to inspect everything but kept her hands in her pockets. The room bore all the marks of Miss Bone—her odd, old-womanish taste, her peculiar collections and ar-rangements. And what was that strange aroma? Poco sniffed the air. It was everywhere in the kitchen—a pungent, salty smell—but seemed to come most powerfully from a large metal pot left cooling on the stove.

The pot loomed well over her head. Poco looked around for something to stand on and discovered a tall stool pushed back into a corner. She dragged it to the stove, climbed up, and peeked over the pot's rim.

Inside, a thick, horrid liquid was still simmering a bit, though the stove had been turned off. Little bubbles swirled against one another and broke into a froth. The stink coming from the pot was so strong now that Poco put her hand over her nose. She was about to climb down when a shadowy movement in the foaming depths below drew her attention. Leaning over the pot again, she saw a pale shape rising toward her. Like a face floating up through dark waters, a single lidless eye surfaced in the center of the brew and, wobbling slightly, fixed its gaze upon her. Poco screamed and toppled backward off the stool.

"IT WAS the Ouija's eye," she gasped to Georgina on the telephone later. "I ran all the way home. I felt it burning into me, watching the whole time I was running."

"The Ouija's eye! Oh, come on. It couldn't have been."

"It was! If you'd seen it, you would have recognized it, too."

"What was it doing in a pot on Miss Bone's stove?"

"I don't know. But I think she's captured the Ouija. It's in her power—like Juliette and the birds and the Harralls' little yard animals. One by one, she's capturing us all."

"Good grief!" Georgina shook her head. "I don't understand any of this."

She glanced around to see where her parents were. Lately it seemed that all the group's most important conversations were taking place on the phone. This was fine for Poco, who was the only child at home and often the only person there at all, since both her parents worked during the day. And it was all right for Walter, because his grandmother rarely even heard the telephone ring. But for Georgina, whose older brother and younger sister and mother and father were right there waiting for their turns, it presented difficulties.

"The main thing to understand is that Miss

Bone is not what she pretends to be," Poco went on in hushed tones. "She is not, and never has been, a nice old teacher. She's probably been getting away with murder for years."

"Oh, dear!" wailed Georgina. "I'm still not sure. I can see how it's possible, but somehow I can't believe it's true."

"It's true," Poco said grimly. "I think she is a witch."

"Oh no!"

"Listen, Georgina, we've got to stop her. I've already talked to Walter, and he agrees that we've got to—"

"Um, Poco? I have to hang up," Georgina whispered. Her father had just come into the room. He began to glare at her and tap his foot.

"Not yet!" exclaimed Poco. "I think we're all in danger. We must be very careful. Don't even think too hard about Miss Bone because she sees into our minds and—"

"I already am in danger," Georgina said, glancing around nervously. Her father had put his hands on his hips and was coming toward her.

"—because Miss Bone knows that I know

about her!" Poco's voice became shrill. "George! Please! You have to help me."

"But I—"

"She knows I know the truth. I'm sure she knows I was in her apartment—"

"I'm sorry but I have to—"

"—and she will try to stop me in any way she can!"

There was the sound of a scuffle at Georgina's end. Her father came on the line.

"Whoever this is, please hang up," he commanded. "Your conversation has gone on far too long."

"But it's important!" Poco couldn't help shrieking. "We've found out something about somebody. Now she's trying to stop us from telling and—"

"Get off! I mean it!" Georgina's father sounded quite angry. Normally such a tone would have shrunk Poco down to fuzzy caterpillar size. The situation was far too desperate for that, however. She gripped the telephone receiver and tried to speak levelly.

"I'm sorry, Mr. Rusk, but I really do need to talk to Georgina for just a minute more. It is very important. I know that if you or Mrs. Rusk had an important telephone call, we would be happy to wait for you while you—"

"Off!" bellowed Mr. Rusk, turning completely rude and unreasonable. He hung up the phone with a crash.

THE NEXT day Poco came down with a terrible cold and had to stay home from school. This was a disaster because Mr. Rusk, in his fury the night before, had forbidden Georgina to use the telephone. She could not call anyone, for any reason, or receive calls, for seven days. It was unfair and mean, but what could anyone do?

Georgina told Walter about it at school. And Walter called Poco to tell her that afternoon. Neither Georgina nor Walter was allowed to visit Poco because she was so contagious. Under these circumstances, the investigators were helpless to protect either themselves or Poco against the rising tide of Miss Bone. There was nothing to do but wait, nervously, to see what happened next—a predicament all too familiar to Walter, apparently.

"Here we are again," he whispered to Georgina

in the hall at school. "It's the story of my life. And now I've dragged you and Poco into the mess."

"Good grief!" Georgina stormed. "That is completely stupid. Nobody drags me anywhere I don't want to go. Why do you think you are the cause of everything?"

Not until the end of the following week could all three meet again, and even then it was not under the best conditions. Poco's cold had cleared up, but a nasty ear infection kept her in bed. She was too dizzy to walk, even to the bathroom, without help. Also, a rash had broken out all over her arms, chest, and face.

"The doctor says it's from my medicine," she said in a wispy voice to Walter and Georgina when, at long last, they were allowed to visit one afternoon. They sat stiffly in chairs across the room from her bed, so as not to catch anything. "He changed me to a new medicine, but I know that's not the real reason I have this rash."

"You certainly are red and bumpy," Georgina said, gazing at the tiny slumped figure. Poco seemed several sizes smaller than the last time they'd seen her. Walter looked quite alarmed and kept pulling his baseball cap on and off at a rapid pace.

"Can I bring you anything?" he asked. "I'm going to talk to somebody about getting you well."

"Please, no," Poco told him. "Don't bring your spirits into this. We're in enough trouble as it is—that's what I'm trying to tell you."

"Oh, I wouldn't worry anymore," Georgina said. "Almost two weeks have gone by since you were in Miss Bone's apartment, and nothing has happened. Juliette hasn't come back, of course, but I really don't think Miss Bone is as bad as you said."

Poco sat up and leaned forward with cold eyes. "But she's worse!" she hissed. "Can't you see what she's doing? She's taking it out on me!"

"On you!" cried Walter and Georgina together.

"That's right," Poco said. She clenched her small fist. "It took me a while, but finally I figured it out. Miss Bone, our deadly enemy, is making me sick."

Nine

"It was when I got this rash, on top of everything else, that I began to suspect her," Poco told the investigators. "Now I know for sure. I can feel Miss Bone working on me. She's taking revenge because of what I saw in her apartment. Don't tell my mother. It would just upset her, and what could she do?"

"Didn't they use to drown witches?" Georgina asked. "Or did they burn them? If you're sure Miss Bone is doing this, we should tell someone. We should go to the police."

"Maybe," Poco said weakly. "I can't think straight anymore."

Walter was staring at her, his pale eyes open

wide. "Telling the police is not a good idea," he said. "I know from experience, you can't fight these kinds of powers. It only makes them madder and they get you in the end. It happened to me."

"What do you mean?" Georgina said. "What did the powers do?"

"Oh, everything." Walter shrugged. "I don't know why, but they picked me out from the very beginning. First they got my parents before I could even talk. Then my aunts and uncles died in different ways. You probably won't believe me, but it's true. Then they got my grandfather, and my cat and my turtle and—"

"Your cat!" cried Poco, coming alive for a moment. "Oh, Walter, that's terrible. I didn't know you had a cat!"

Walter nodded mournfully. "I'm the only one left in my family now. Except for my grandmother. And they could get her with one little push if they wanted. She's so old. I worry about her all the time, but I pretend not to. Whenever I worry or try to stop them, the spirits close in and hit me again. It's gotten so I'm afraid to walk down the street because something might happen. Remember, I was the one who was watching when—"

"Juliette was run over!" cried Poco. "Oh, Walter, how horrible. I never understood before. I thought you were just strange, or shy, or . . ."

"Crazy," Georgina finished in an irritated voice. She frowned at Walter. "This is ridiculous! Juliette was not run over because you were watching. It was an accident."

Walter shook his head gloomily. "That's how the spirits make it look so I can't pin it on them. But they're doing it, all right. Who else that you know has had so much bad stuff happen to him?"

Poco nodded. "I never knew why you crept around the way you do."

"I try to be invisible," Walter said. "I keep hoping the bad spirits will forget about me and go off someplace else. Thank goodness for the good spirits to help balance the bad ones out. The Ouija board is on my side. It was what told me I was on the hit list in the beginning. Up to then, I couldn't figure out what was going on."

"I think the Ouija board is on nobody's side," Georgina said. "It sees and tells. It doesn't care."

"But it warned us about our deadly enemy," Walter reminded her.

"Until it fell under the deadly enemy's power itself," Poco went on. "Slowly but surely, Miss Bone is closing in."

All three were silent at this, and a hopeless feeling of entrapment circled among them. Or rather, it circled between Poco and Walter, who gazed limply at each other across the bedroom. Georgina had another sort of look in her eye.

"I can't stand this!" she exclaimed at last, jumping to her feet. "I can't sit around being invisible while some witch or evil spirit closes in for the kill. I have to go on with the investigation."

"But you can't," Poco said. "The investigation is over. We know everything. It's just a matter of what to do."

"I'm not so sure," Georgina said. "I'd like to pay a visit to Miss Bone first. I want to hear what she has to say. There must be a reason why she's doing all this."

"Miss Bone!" Poco turned white. "But you can't!" she shrieked. "People like her don't have reasons. She'll come after you. Or she'll put some even worse sickness into me. Oh, please,

Georgina. Don't do it, please. I'm so weak already, I couldn't bear any more."

Walter, also, was appalled by the idea. He ran over to Poco's bedside to try to calm her. But Georgina stood firm and would not change her mind. She could be absolutely impossible when she wanted to be.

When they saw how determined Georgina was to throw herself into the clutches of the unknown, Poco and Walter drew themselves up. They knew they could not let her go alone. Alone, she would be helpless. Like Juliette, she might never come back.

"All right!" Walter said. "We'll go together to visit Miss Bone. She will have a hard time getting rid of all of us at once."

"She wouldn't do it that way," Poco warned. "She'd take her time and make it look natural. You know, Walter, I wonder if Miss Bone is at the bottom of everything—even your parents. Whatever way we turn, there she is staring at us like the horrible Ouija eye."

This was a fascinating idea, but the investigators did not have time to think about it more deeply. Georgina, having decided what to do, now wanted to do it, immediately! So Poco crawled out of bed and staggered into her clothes while Walter went downstairs to make sure the coast was clear. Mrs. Lambert had been forced to go back to work for a few hours that afternoon, which was why the friends had been allowed to come over to begin with. They would have just enough time to whisk Poco out of the house.

And whisk her they did because she was still too dizzy to walk. Walter carried her piggyback as far as the bus stop. Then Georgina took over for the rest of the way. Poco was so thin and small that she hardly weighed anything, except for her winter coat. The afternoon was cold. In Poco's pale cheeks, a faint rosiness appeared, giving her a look of health she hadn't had for many days.

"Oh, it's so nice to be out!" she exclaimed once, but afterward became solemn again.

"There's Angela's house," Georgina said when the big, elegant structure loomed up ahead. "And there's the garage."

"Is Miss Bone home?" Walter asked, in a voice that showed how much he wished she were not.

"It's hard to tell. She usually parks in the ga-rage."

They walked straight down the driveway, a means of approach strange to them all. Though they knew they were at risk, each felt a flash of relief when passing by their chilly hideout in the bushes. It was so much better to be out taking action.

Georgina let Poco down gently on Miss Bone's famous stone stoop. There was nothing on it now, though the bodies of the little animals had made such an impression on Poco that for a moment she imagined she saw them again. She huddled against Walter while Georgina pushed the button that rang the doorbell. Far away, in some eerie recess of Miss Bone's apartment, a chime went off. A door opened above. Footsteps came slowly down toward them.

"Hello? Yes, what is it?" Miss Bone's frightful old face peered out. Her eyes dug deep into Poco at once. "My goodness, child! You look thoroughly ill. Come in, all of you, and get out of the cold. Whatever it is, I'll take care of you upstairs."

Ten

AND NOW, with a charm too powerful to resist, Miss Bone guided the little group up her dim staircase. She drew them like flies into the webby depths of her witch's chambers. Poco's heart had never beat so hard. Walter's hand was frozen in a sort of salute near the brim of his cap. Even Georgina had to catch her breath when she stepped into Miss Bone's kitchen and saw with her own eyes everything that Poco had described over the phone.

There were the aprons and the yellowed lace, the baskets and the tea and coffee jars, the herbs and grasses and—oh! (Georgina jumped in spite of herself)—the same tall stool that Poco had climbed upon to peer over the edge of the big pot.

And there was the stove! Georgina turned toward it, ready to gasp if the pot should still be there. It wasn't. A blackened teakettle squatted on one of the burners instead. It was to this that Miss Bone now turned her attention.

"Of course, you must have some tea," she said, grasping the handle with a faint smile. Or was she frowning? Her face was so wrinkly it was hard to tell. "You look raw and cold as polar penguins!"

She filled the kettle at the sink and set it back on the stove. "Not that polar penguins really *are* cold, since they are born on ice and live on ice and have never known anything else. Only we who look at them think they must be cold," Miss Bone went on, turning up the gas burner, "because we would be cold if we were in their shoes. Or should I say 'in their flippers'? We so often misunderstand the ways of creatures different from us."

The investigators stared at her with unblinking eyes. Their minds were a perfect blank. Whether this was a result of their own fright at being so close to the enemy, or of Miss Bone's terrible magic, there was no telling. She gave them a sharp-toothed smile, opened a cupboard, and looked inside.

"Ladyfingers," she announced. "I'm afraid that's all I have for sweets."

Poco chose this moment to sag toward the floor. Walter caught her just in time.

"Heavens, child!" Miss Bone cried out. "Go into the living room and lie down on the couch."

"N-n-no, thank you," Walter said. "We'll just stay here, all together, if you don't mind. We have to be leaving in a minute, anyway." He glanced at the door, as if he were afraid it might seal over and disappear.

"Well, suit yourselves," Miss Bone said. She gestured toward several chairs surrounding the tiny kitchen table. "But I must tell you that I have no intention of letting you go home just yet. No one who enters my kitchen gets away so easily as that!"

Georgina and Walter exchanged terrified looks, and Poco's legs gave out completely at this. Walter lowered her carefully into one of the kitchen chairs and sank down beside her. Georgina sat across from them, perched in the upright position of a rocket ship waiting to be launched.

It was now time that somebody in the group should speak up and begin to question Miss Bone. No one seemed able to utter a word, though. The old teacher had boiled the tea water, poured it into a china teapot, brought cups and saucers and spoons and napkins and sugar and milk to the table, and sat down herself before the silence was broken. Then it was she who spoke.

"Well!" She opened her vein-choked hands as if to conjure another spell. "I'm so pleased you've come to visit me at last! I've been watching you, you know. Oh yes, I've had my eye on you. . . ."

Poco felt ill. A queer white mist kept rising around the edges of her vision. She wondered if she would faint and decided she must not. The danger was too great. She clung dizzily to her chair and stared at Miss Bone. The old witch was chattering away, pretending to be a normal person as she poured out the tea. It reminded Poco of Walter's spirits.

"That's how they make it look so I can't pin it on them," he'd told Georgina about the accidents that were always happening around him.

Poco knew that Miss Bone was playing the same game.

The old woman handed her a cup of tea. She had been round to all three of them, asking their names and what families they came from. She remembered Poco's brother in her English class. She and Walter's grandmother had known each other years ago.

"So you are Walter Kew," she said, gazing at him curiously. "I remember you as a baby. You arrived in a most unexpected way."

"I did?" Walter said. No one had ever told him this before.

Miss Bone shook her head and went back to pouring tea.

"At first, I couldn't imagine what you children were doing out there in the bushes," she said, handing Georgina and Walter their cups. "Do you take sugar? Milk?" Her eyes darted back and forth over them.

"Then I understood. You were looking for the lost cat. I heard it had run away. Perhaps you thought I'd given it shelter? I suppose I should have come right out and told you I hadn't, but . . . truthfully, I rather liked having you there."

Miss Bone gave them a small smile. "I kept

hoping you'd decide to come inside and visit me. And now you have!" She chuckled with pleasure. "I don't get many young visitors anymore. This is such a treat for an old teacher!"

Miss Bone looked brightly at the investigators, as if she expected them to believe her.

"So you haven't seen Juliette at all—is that what you're saying?" Georgina said, speaking at last in a high, nervous voice.

"Is that the kitty's name?" Miss Bone shrugged her shoulders. "No, not a whisker!"

"And you haven't done anything with her all this time she's been lost?"

"Done anything with her? What would I have done?" Miss Bone looked confused, then offended. "Did you think I'd hurt her?"

"We weren't sure," Georgina said.

Miss Bone's expression turned serious. "I see. Well, there was one evening when I thought something might have been about. I came out for a breath of air and found some little dead mice and moles lying on my front stoop. 'Aha!' I said. 'What else but a cat would make such a collection?' I brought the poor little bodies inside and put out a bowl of milk in exchange. But nothing came to drink it, that night or the next.

Whatever had been here must have gone off somewhere else."

Poco scowled, but Georgina's chin lifted a bit. She leaned forward to ask another question.

"What did you do with the mice and moles?"

An embarrassed look came over Miss Bone's face. "If you must know, I wrapped them in little napkins and put them in the refrigerator. Then the next morning I took them outside and tucked them down in the dirt under the hedge. I suppose it's silly, but I've always believed in proper burials. Mice, moles, or men—everyone's entitled to respect in the end, I always say."

Georgina's expression softened after this, as did Walter's. Even Poco glanced up in surprise. But a moment later her eyes narrowed again.

"A large pot?" Miss Bone was saying, in answer to Georgina's next question. "Here? Goodness, what an investigation this is. You make me feel like a criminal."

She glanced at them nervously. "I cook soups from time to time in such a pot as you've described. I'm not fond of canned soup, especially the chowders. Why pay all that money for ready-made when it's so easy to boil up a few fish heads and carcasses into good fish stock? Add cream, potatoes, and onions, and you're on your way. Is that a good-enough answer?"

"Fish heads!" Georgina exclaimed. She turned toward Walter. "Good grief, we never thought of that!"

"Thought of what!" Miss Bone exclaimed. "I demand to know what I am being accused of."

Walter cleared his throat. "Ahem . . . do these fish heads ever happen to have . . . um . . . open eyes?"

"They always have them," Miss Bone said. "That's how they come. Why?"

"Oh, dear," Walter muttered. He looked at her unhappily over Poco's head.

"You cooked up a fish chowder not too long ago, didn't you?" Georgina asked. "A week ago last Tuesday, I think it might have been."

Miss Bone was astonished. "Why, yes, I did," she said. "But how would you know? Or perhaps I see." Her face sagged suddenly. "Your investigation."

Georgina nodded.

Miss Bone looked away. There was a pause while she groped first in one pocket, then more desperately in another.

"Well!" she said finally, with a brave attempt at

brightness. "And here I'd managed to convince myself that you'd come to make friends. My goodness, how a fool can fool herself when she wants to. Of course, you needn't stay a minute longer, any of you. What a horror I must seem to you. Off you go. It's quite all right. Don't worry about the teacups. I'll clear them up later."

She fumbled in yet another pocket and this time drew out a rumpled bit of tissue. "Don't mind me," cried Miss Bone, pressing her nose into the tissue. "I believe I'm coming down with a terrible cold!"

Georgina sat still for a moment, watching the old woman. Then, to Poco's fright, she leaned forward and took Miss Bone's leathery hand in hers.

"Oh, Miss Bone, don't be upset. We've been wrong about you. We are so sorry. Somehow we got the idea that you'd kidnapped Juliette."

"Kidnapped her! Good gracious. What would the Harralls think!" Miss Bone turned around and glared at them.

"And that you were controlling things in an evil way. Walter's Ouija board gave us false ir formation."

Even Walter nodded to this.

"Did you say Ouija board?" Miss Bone sniffed. "I used to have one of those. It always seemed to tell me exactly what I suspected."

"We got off on a strange track, all right," Georgina agreed. "Poco sneaked into your apartment once while you were out. She was absolutely sure you were a w—"

Miss Bone glanced toward Poco. "Good heavens!" she cried out, before Georgina could finish. "The child has turned as white as a sheet. Quick, help me carry her into the living room."

Together they all reached for Poco, whose head was listing dangerously to one side. They caught her body just as it was about to collapse onto the floor and lifted her and carried her in to the couch.

"Put her legs up on cushions!" Miss Bone ordered. "We must get the blood running back into her head. Walter, fill a glass with water and bring it here. Georgina, dampen a dish towel under the faucet and lay it on her forehead. We'll bring her around."

Miss Bone mopped her own wrinkled forehead and gazed at Poco in real distress.

"The poor little thing is so skinny and exhausted. She's been sick, if I am not mistaken.

She should have been in a bed all this time, not gallivanting about in the cold. I certainly will not allow her to go back home with you," she told the others.

"You won't?" Walter asked.

"No!"

"But . . . she'll want to go!"

"So she will, but I won't allow it."

"But you can't keep her here forever!" cried Walter, his worst suspicions about Miss Bone rising up again.

"Of course not," she said with a teacherish snap. "I am going to call Mrs. Lambert and tell her to come get this poor child right now in her car. I would drive her home myself if my old broomstick weren't having one of its evil spells. The blasted thing wouldn't start for anything this morning!"

Miss Bone gave the friends such an accusing stare that Walter blushed and Georgina lowered her head in shame. Then the old lady rose and strode nobly into the kitchen toward the telephone.

Eleven

MRS. LAMBERT came quickly to pick up Poco that cold afternoon. She was at the door not five minutes after Miss Bone had called, much to Georgina's surprise.

"My mother would have taken an hour at least," she whispered to Walter. "Thirty minutes if I'd been run over by a truck."

"Don't say that," hissed Walter. "You never know who's listening!"

"I suppose it comes from being the only child left at home," Georgina went on in longing tones. They both watched as Mrs. Lambert smoothed the hair off her daughter's forehead and bent to give her a kiss.

"Not necessarily," Walter said. "My grandmother never comes for me. She's so old they took her driver's license away. I have to call a taxi."

"A taxi!" Georgina gazed at him with admiration. Lately she'd found herself beginning to like this nervous, wiry person.

Poco had recovered by now and was sitting up on Miss Bone's couch with a blanket around her shoulders. She looked pale but otherwise herself again.

"You know," said Mrs. Lambert, squeezing onto the couch beside her, "maybe it was a good thing to get you out of the house for a while. From what I can see, your rash has disappeared!"

"It has?" Poco examined herself. "Well . . . so it has."

"How does your head feel? Still spinning a bit?"

Poco cocked her head and squinted across the room. "It's better," she admitted, then frowned as if she wished it weren't.

"Aha!" Miss Bone exclaimed. "That's my special chamomile tea at work. Look, she's drunk nearly the whole cup. Chamomile seems to fix almost anything."

"Chamomile tea?" Poco's mother beamed. "My grandmother used to make that for me when I was sick."

"Oh, it's a grandmother's remedy, all right," Miss Bone agreed. "One of those things considered strange in this day and age for no other reason than that it's been around so long." She winked at Poco. "Look at this child! She already appears well enough to walk by herself to the car."

"Of course I can walk!" Poco said crossly. She threw off the blanket, stood up, and began to put on her coat.

Walter and Georgina put on their coats, too. Mrs. Lambert had offered to drop them off at their houses on her way home. Then they turned and smiled at Miss Bone and apologized again for what they had believed. (But Georgina saw Poco scowl.) Miss Bone invited them to return soon, when she would have better supplies on hand, including Scottish scones and shortbread "and other recipes of mine from the dark ages," she joked. "Your grandmother will know them, Walter. She was quite a cook in her day."

"She was?"

"Casseroles were her specialty. I remember that she had the biggest casserole dish in town and used to cook for fifty or more for our church suppers. In fact, that's how you first—" She stopped and put her hand over her mouth.

"How I first what?" Walter demanded. Here was something else he had never heard before. "Did you know my parents?" he asked her suspiciously. Miss Bone shook her head.

"Leave the past to the past," she advised him, and changed the subject. "Is everyone ready to go? I'll show you downstairs. Watch your step, my dears. Farewell! See you soon! But . . . where is Poco?"

They all looked around. She seemed to have stayed behind in Miss Bone's apartment.

"I'll get her!" cried Walter. He ran back up and found her in a corner of the kitchen. She was staring at a wooden peg, upon which hung a large gray fur hat.

"Poco, it isn't what you think!"

"Why are you so sure?" Poco pushed his hand off her arm.

"Because I am. Miss Bone is just old and different from other people. When you get to know her, you can see she's not a witch. Come on."

"You go ahead," Poco said. She waited until he was all the way downstairs again before walking down herself and getting into the front seat of her mother's car.

So the extraordinary afternoon came to an end. Walter and Georgina climbed into the car also. They sat together in the backseat gazing thoughtfully out the windows. The facts of Miss Bone had been so whirled and changed before their eyes that they were still not entirely sure what had happened. They had the oddest feeling that they'd been under some enchantment but were now woken up to the real world again.

"Everything looks so different!" Georgina exclaimed. Her eyes had never been so sharp. Angela's yard was as lovely as a painting. She saw a squirrel sprint up a tree.

"And so bright," Walter added. "I feel as if I've been trapped in a cave and have finally been allowed to crawl out in the sun. Do you think some spirit put a spell on us and all this time we've been in its power?"

"Your horrible Ouija eye—that's what started

everything," Georgina replied. "I'd get rid of it, if I were you. Its magic is too strong; it changes who you are. Poco, are you all right?"

In front of her, Poco had slumped down in the front seat. Only the topmost hairs of her head showed above it. When they leaned forward to investigate, Walter and Georgina discovered that her eyes were closed. There was nothing wrong, though. She had only fallen asleep.

THE WEEK following the investigators' daring visit to Miss Bone's apartment was so wild and woolly with the coming holidays that there was no time to think of what had happened. At school, it was the week before winter vacation, which meant pageants and singing programs, costumes and decorations, and strange things served for lunch that the kitchen crew invented.

"Green french fries?" Georgina muttered, gazing in amazement at her tray in the lunchroom.

Walter sat down across from her with his paper bag. "What is that fuzzy thing sitting on top of your hamburger?" he asked.

"A Santa Claus hat. All the hamburgers have them today," Georgina said, then sighed. "Too bad Poco's missing this," she added, for Poco still had not returned to school. "I heard she had to give up her solo in the music program. She was going to sing 'White Christmas,' but Mrs. Henderson turned it over to Julia Francis instead."

"Julia Francis! That screecher? Poco will be furious."

"She already is furious. But not about that. She's furious at us because she thinks we double-crossed her."

Walter slumped in his chair. "I know. She won't talk to me on the phone. When she hears my voice, she hangs up. Why doesn't she get well and come back to school?"

"Because she is Poco and thinks she's right," Georgina said. "And because she's right, she refuses to get well because if she got well it would prove she was wrong. She still believes that Miss Bone has put a hex on her and is keeping Juliette prisoner."

"Poor old Miss Bone! It's so unfair. What's wrong with Poco? I always thought she was a reasonable type of person."

"No one is a reasonable type of person. Not one person on this planet," Georgina replied with a flick of her fork. "The older you get, the more you see that. The trouble with Poco is she can't face up to Juliette being dead, so she's decided to believe in spells. You should understand, Walter. It's the same with your spirits."

"What do you mean!" he protested. "My spirits are real!"

"Hah!" said Georgina with such a piercing glance that he looked away. Luckily her mind was not really on him, though. "Let's walk over and see Poco this afternoon," she said. "We should try to talk to her."

"She won't want to see us."

"Let's go, anyway. She has to stop pretending sometime that Juliette is coming back. Otherwise, she'll just get crazier and crazier."

For some reason, this remark seemed to unsettle Walter even more than the one before. He pulled his cap down over his eyes and refused to say another word during all the rest of lunch.

AT FIRST when they knocked on the Lamberts' front door, everyone seemed to be out. Only after repeated pounding and ringing, and some yelling on the part of Georgina, did a small movement in a second-floor window catch their eyes. The curtains inside were parted. A face gazed out. A few seconds later soft footsteps could be heard coming down the stairs. The door was pulled open by . . .

"Poco!" Georgina cried. "How great that you're up. We know you don't want to see us, but here we are so maybe we could come in anyway?"

Georgina placed a determined foot over the threshold. Behind her stood Walter, slouched down and shuffling.

Poco stared at them. She was wearing a pretty rose-colored nightgown. Her expression wasn't angry. It was blank.

"So, anyway," Georgina went on, "we've been having the most amazing things for lunch at school. We thought you'd like to hear. If we could just come in. Aren't you cold standing in the door like this?"

Poco continued to stare at them. Georgina felt unnerved. Had something already gone wrong in Poco's head? She looked odd. Georgina put her other foot through the door and more or less forced her way in. Walter followed with a hop and a scuttle.

"So, anyway!" roared Georgina, who tended to speak more loudly the more nervous she was. "How's everything? Is your mom at work? Are you getting better?"

Poco closed the door behind them. She turned around and gave them the sweetest smile. When Georgina opened her mouth to roar again, she raised a finger to her lips, over the smile, and beckoned.

"Come upstairs, please," she whispered. "An amazing thing has happened."

"An amazing thing?" Georgina bellowed.

"Ssh!"

They followed Poco up the stairs, down the hall, into her bedroom. There on the foot of her bed lay Miss Bone's beautiful gray fur hat in a tremendous mound.

Georgina jumped. "Good grief!"

Walter backed away.

Poco positively beamed. "Isn't it wonderful?" she asked. "Just where she always used to sleep."

Georgina looked at her friend in horror. "Oh, Poco," she began, and would have thrown her arms around the little figure and put her to bed at once, a person as sick in the head as that. But suddenly something impossible occurred. The fur hat twitched. One furry edge broke free of the mound and rose up in the air like a wisp of smoke.

Then, as Georgina and Walter watched, the hat began to unfold. A pair of ears developed in its middle; a pink nose appeared. Two blue eyes blinked open amid the fur. A long paw stretched out in a leisurely way, and the whole hat turned into an enormous yawning cat.

Georgina would have screamed if she could, but no sound came out. Walter fell into the chair across the room that was provided for visitors.

"It's a miracle, isn't it?" Poco asked them. "Juliette came back this morning. She just scratched at the door, and we let her in."

Twelve

NEVER HAD anything seemed so impossible as Juliette's return to the Lamberts' house. After all, she had been gone almost a month. No one in the neighborhood had seen her during all that time. Bowls of milk and food left out had never been touched. Snow had fallen. Winds had howled. Temperatures had plunged to icy depths. There was no way an old run-over cat could have lived through it.

"I thought it was Miss Bone's hat," Georgina kept gasping. "I can't believe it's Juliette. Juliette was hit by a car. She was dead."

"Well, she's risen back up," Poco said proudly, "just the way I knew she would. I never lost *my* belief." She lifted her chin in Georgina's direction.

"Glad to meet you at last, Juliette," Walter said. He went across the room to shake her paw. "I only saw you from a distance the first time. You were in midair, not looking too good."

Juliette smiled up at him and began to wash her whiskers.

"She certainly looks fine now," Georgina said, leaning forward to inspect her more closely. "Wait a minute! This does not look like a cat that's been huddling in the cold. This looks like a cat that's been lying around on silk pillows in an expensive hotel."

"And eating tons of tuna fish," Walter added, stroking her well-padded back.

"And having her coat washed and her nails clipped. Look!" said Georgina, holding up a well-groomed paw.

"And her ears and tail fluffed."

"Juliette, where have you been all this time?" Georgina asked, bending down to look into the cat's deep blue eyes. "What have you been doing?"

Poco had kept silent during all this questioning. Finally she spoke up.

"Juliette hasn't been at a hotel. She became an invisible and went to another world."

"Became a *what*?" Georgina's eyes narrowed.

"Don't act so surprised, George. You said yourself that's probably where she was."

"I did not! I never said that. I was only making a joke to your mother."

"Well, you were right." Poco nodded wisely. "Juliette and I had a long talk today. She told me everything."

"Good grief!" shouted Georgina. "I can't stand this!"

"Well, you will have to stand it because it's true," Poco said in her most maddening voice. "A leader of the invisibles invited Juliette to come. She happened to be passing by and saw Juliette in trouble with the car. So she just swooped down and carried her off. Wasn't that nice?"

Georgina's eyes were fiery. "I hope you told Juliette about all the trouble we got into trying to find her. How Walter's Ouija tricked us, and Miss Bone became our deadly enemy, how she started making you sick and boiling eyes and eating little animals!"

Poco lowered her head as Georgina said these things. An ashamed look came over her face.

"I'm so sorry. I see now how wrong I was."

"You do?" asked Walter, in surprise. "But how? What happened?"

"Juliette told me everything," Poco replied, while Georgina gritted her teeth. "We are both going to see Miss Bone right away. I will apologize. Do you know what a dreadful thing we did?"

Georgina was gazing furiously at the ceiling.

"I see it all now—thanks to Juliette, of course," Poco went on. "We accused Miss Bone of being a witch, but we were really the witches. We changed her into something she never was. It doesn't matter that we thought we were right. Juliette said there's no room in the world for excuses like that. Witches like us are dangerous. Don't forget how they burned those poor people in Salem."

This was such a clear picture of exactly what they had done to Miss Bone that Georgina was astounded. Poco had made an impossible leap. "Who told you all this?" she shouted at her. "I know it wasn't Juliette."

"It most certainly was."

"Well, I don't believe it."

"Well, you will," Poco announced, "when I show you this last incredible thing."

"What?" cried Walter and Georgina together.

With practiced hands, Poco lifted Juliette up in the air and gathered her together in a furry lump on her lap. Then she smoothed back the rather too-thick hair around the cat's neck to reveal a narrow sparkling band. Everyone leaned forward to look. It seemed to be woven out of a sort of thin silver rope. Threaded here and there on the strands were tiny glass beads that glittered in the light whenever Juliette tossed her head.

"This was on her when she came back," Poco said, sounding rather in awe herself. "My mother can't imagine where it came from. And there's something else. A charm."

It swung suddenly into view, a small square metal box that hung by a link from the silver collar. Georgina's eyes had turned bright and enchanted.

"Have you looked inside?"

"Yes."

"Well, what's in it?"

Poco smiled. "Catnip," she said. "It's a precious gift, all right. Who else but an invisible would think of such a thing?"

She unlatched the tiny box with careful fingers and allowed them to bend near. A strong minty smell rose from a mixture inside that looked like dried leaves. Walter drew back and sneezed.

"So that's what catnip smells like. Tickly," Georgina said. "But why did the invisibles put it on Juliette?"

"To protect her, of course," Poco replied. She latched the box shut and hugged the old cat closer. "They put a spell on this catnip to keep Juliette safe. From now on she can only live the longest, happiest life."

From the moment of Juliette's return, the group began to settle down. No longer were they a cart rolling wildly along on two wheels. A new balance sprang up among them, and whether this had to do with Juliette being home, or the little box of catnip, or a sense they all had that some unknown power, partly good and partly dangerous, had been working silently behind the scenes, no one could say.

To begin with, Georgina no longer felt angry at Poco.

"I don't even care that she's talking to squirrels and birds again," she told Walter. "I'm not asking any questions about where she gets her ideas. I'm just glad to have the old Poco back. There are some people you shouldn't try to change."

On her side, Poco recovered from Georgina's insulting remarks and even went so far as to thank her for dragging them all to Miss Bone.

"If you hadn't been so completely rude and horrible, we never would have gone," Poco said. "And then we never would have found out how wrong we were."

"You mean how wrong you were," Georgina said, pressing her advantage.

"No, that's not what I mean."

"Well, that's what you should mean!"

(They could still disagree about small matters, unfortunately.)

Meanwhile, Poco called Angela and told her the whole story, and Angela called Georgina to hear what really happened, and they all felt quite close together again.

"When *are* you coming back?" Georgina asked Angela. "There's a lot to investigate around here. The unknown keeps popping up all over the place and we are beginning to forget what you look like."

At this, Angela started to sniff and blow her nose. By the time she hung up, she had developed a terrible cold.

"Maybe it's not so great down in Mexico as she's been saying," Georgina told Poco.

Walter Kew was the only one in the group who seemed uneasy about things. Daily he followed Poco and Georgina about, as if he were afraid they might disappear before his eyes. But since they had grown quite fond of him, it was no bother at all.

"Do you think I'm getting crazier?" he asked Georgina one afternoon when all three of them were trudging home from school. The winter vacation was over by that time. Mid-January was upon them—ice, snow, and all.

"Crazier than what?" Georgina said.

"Well, than I was before."

"Were you crazy before?"

"A little," Walter said. "You would have been, too, with all those spirits circling around waiting to pounce on you. Ever since Juliette came back, it's been better, though. I think they may finally be moving on to someone else."

"I hope it's not me," Georgina said. "Or Poco." They both looked back at her. She had stopped to examine some bird footprints in the snow.

"I've given up using the Ouija board, too," Walter said. "After poor Miss Bone, I couldn't trust it again. There's got to be a better way of figuring out the world."

"So why are you getting crazier?" Georgina asked. "You sound perfectly fine to me."

"It's my parents." Walter shook his head dismally. "I know I should leave the past to the past, but I can't help it. I think about them. I wish I could talk to them and find out what happened. I keep wondering if they are somewhere, looking down at me. They wouldn't completely disappear, would they? Maybe they miss me. Oh, it's crazy, I know."

"Didn't Miss Bone know something about you?"

"She wouldn't tell."

"Don't give up that easily." Georgina snorted. "This sounds like something that needs to be investigated."

"It does?" Walter said, brightening. "Well, yes, I guess it does. For some strange reason, I never thought of it that way."

Poco caught up with them then and made a great fuss over a robin she'd just been talking to who was trying a new experiment of not flying south.

"He wants to know the effect of winter on the robin body—besides cold feet, of course. That goes without saying."

"Of course," sighed Georgina.

"So far, the worst thing has been having no one to talk to," Poco went on. "He says he's been quite lonely since all his friends left."

"That's sad," Walter said. "Who would guess that even birds can get lonely."

Poco nodded. "So he was wondering if we'd mind if he tagged along with us for a while. He likes groups. It's what he's used to."

"Tag along!" exclaimed Georgina. "Where *is* this bird?"

"Up there."

They all looked up into a tree overhead. Sitting on an icy branch was a robin who cocked his head at them and then looked away.

"Good grief!" Georgina exploded. "I can't believe it!"

"You never believe anything," Poco said. "That is the trouble with you."

"Well, you believe in everything, whether it's true or not."

"No, I don't."

"Yes, you do!"

This appeared to be the sort of argument that might go on for several hours, so Walter stepped away. He pulled his cap down hard over his eyes and struck out by himself for another part of town. It seemed as good a time as any to begin a new investigation.